First published in Great Britain in 2022 by Andersen Press Ltd.,
20 Vauxhall Bridge Road, London, SW1V 2SA, UK
Vijverlaan 48, 3062 HL Rotterdam, Nederland
Copyright © David McKee, 2022.
The right of David McKee to be identified as the author and
illustrator of this work has been asserted by him in accordance
with the Copyright, Designs and Patents Act, 1988.
All rights reserved.
Colour separated in Switzerland by Photolitho AG, Zürich.
Printed and bound in China.
1   3   5   7   9   10   8   6   4   2
British Library Cataloguing in Publication Data available.
ISBN 978 1 83913 159 2

ELMER
and the Gift

David McKee

Ⓐ

Andersen Press

Elmer the patchwork elephant was walking one of
his walks when he saw his young friend, Rose.
"Hello, Rose," called Elmer.
"Hello, Elmer," Rose answered, "I've just seen
Aunt Zelda, she's looking for you."

"Aunt Zelda?" asked Elmer. "Perhaps we'd better find her, she's a bit deaf and forgets things. Come on."

"Elmer," called a voice. It was Tiger.
"Aunt Zelda is looking for you, she has something to give you.
I say, Elmer, it isn't Christmas, is it?"
"Maybe just for Aunt Zelda," said Elmer.

A moment later, two monkeys called, "Hi Elmer!"
"Aunt Zelda is looking for you," said one. "She has
something to give you. Is it your birthday?"
"No," said Elmer, "but Aunt Zelda may think it is."

"Something to give you," said Rose as they continued.
"I love presents. Look, there is Aunt Zelda."

"Hello, Aunt Zelda," said Rose and Elmer together.
"I think you were looking for me," said Elmer.
"Did he really, Dear?" said Aunt Zelda.
"Poor old Lion."

As they walked on, Elmer wondered what Aunt
Zelda thought that he had said.

She continued, "I'm glad that we met, there's something I have to give you, Elmer. But I can't remember what it is or where it is."

"Perhaps we can jog your memory," said Elmer.
"Is it big?"

"A pig?" said Aunt Zelda. "What a funny idea. Imagine Old Eldo giving me a pig to give you."

"Oh so it's something from Grandpa Eldo," said Rose.
"Let's go and see him," said Elmer. "It's not far."
"No, Dear," said Aunt Zelda. "It would be best if we just went to see Eldo, it's not far."
"Good idea," said Elmer.

It wasn't long before they were with
Grandpa Eldo.
"This is a nice surprise," he said.
"Grandpa Eldo," said Elmer, "we have a problem
and you can help us to solve it. You asked Aunt
Zelda to give me something and now she can't
remember what it is or where it is."

"Give you something?" said Eldo. "Let me think now. Oh, yes. Of course. I said, 'If you see Elmer, give him my love.'"

"I remember now," said Zelda. "It was love."

"Ah! Love," said Rose, "that's nice."
"Fantastic," said Elmer, "and I love all of you."
"Really?" said Aunt Zelda. "Well maybe it does but never on a Thursday."